MASTERS OF THE GENIE

First published in the United States
of America in 1989 by The Mallard Press

Mallard Press and its accompanying design
and logo are trademarks of BDD Promotional
Book Company, Inc.

Produced by
Twin Books
15 Sherwood Place
Greenwich, CT 06830

ISBN 0-792-45235-6

Printed in Hong Kong

Twin Books

MALLARD PRESS

The news spread quickly. Scrooge McDuck was somewhere in Arabia, looking for Aladdin's Magic Lamp. Huey, Dewey and Louie had gone along for the adventure.

"Come on, lads," said Uncle Scrooge. "Accordin' to the map, Aladdin's cave is right around here."

Suddenly, a loud boom made the mountain shake. The ground opened up and swallowed Scrooge! Down, down he fell. Luckily for him, his hiking rope was still tied to a rock. He swung just above the ground.

Scrooge looked around. "Bless me bagpipes!" he whispered. He was face to face with the famous Magic Lamp of Aladdin. But he was also face to face with his rival, Flintheart Glomgold.

4

"Glomgold!" yelled Scrooge, "I'll bet you're the one who blasted the cave open."

"Naturally," said Glomgold. "I've come for the lamp!"

"Oh, no, you don't! It's mine!" cried Scrooge. They both grabbed the lamp.

Thick yellow smoke rose from the lamp and turned into a very fat person. "I'm the Genie of the Lamp," he said. "Which one of you is my master? I can make three of your wishes come true!"

"I am!" said Glomgold.

"No! I am!" said Scrooge.

"Since you cannot agree, you must settle this with a contest," said the Genie. "You will both race from here to your homes. The first one home will win the lamp."

"That's not fair!" said Glomgold. "I live farther away than Scrooge. Let's race to the Hot Ice Cream Parlor in Duckburg. Agreed?"

By now, Huey, Dewey and Louie were standing next to their uncle.

"What should we do?" asked Dewey.

"Take the Genie home with you and wait," ordered Scrooge.

"What a wonderful idea!" said the Genie.

So Scrooge and Glomgold started their trek toward Duckburg.

Meanwhile, in a blink, the Genie and Scrooge's nephews were at Scrooge's mansion.

But bringing the Genie home was a bad idea. He drove the cook crazy, ordering huge meals. He kept the butler busy running errands. He took over the swimming pool. And he sat in front of the television for hours.

The Genie was in no hurry to grant anyone's three wishes. Then he would be stuck in the Magic Lamp again.

"This place is much nicer than my lamp," he thought to himself. "I'm going to make sure Scrooge and Glomgold take a long time to get back to Duckburg!"

The Genie waved his hand over the television set, and there were Scrooge and Glomgold, right on the screen! The Genie watched them march across the desert, and smiled an evil smile.

Both Scrooge and Glomgold wanted to get to Duckburg first. Neither one would let the other get ahead—not even by a foot. Racing to keep up with each other, they sweated under the hot sun.

They were so busy trying to outrun each other that they didn't notice they were running in circles. They were under the magic spell of the Genie.

The Genie laughed as he watched them run in circles. Then he had another mean idea.

"I'll send them back in time," he said to himself, "back to the days of Barr-Aba-Sada and its cruel Sultan."

Once again the Genie snapped his fingers, and a sandstorm rose up around Scrooge and Glomgold. When the storm died down, they were in front of an ancient Arabian city.

"A city!" they cried. "That means help!"

But when they reached the city, Scrooge and Glomgold were surrounded by soldiers carrying sharp spears. Without a word, the soldiers marched them to the Sultan's palace.

"What are you doing here?" demanded the Sultan. "Barr-Aba-Sada is a forbidden city. You must be spies!"

"No, no! You are wrong!" cried Scrooge. "We are lost in this desert. We only want to find our way home."

"A likely story," laughed the cruel Sultan. He turned to the lady next to him. "Don't you agree, Sherwebazad?"

"They are strangers," said the lady. "Perhaps they really do not know that it is forbidden to visit our city."

"Please help us!" begged Glomgold.

"Enough! Take them to the crocodile pit!" ordered the Sultan.

The guards led them to a dark cell with a pool in the center. Scrooge was thirsty, and he bent down to take a drink. Suddenly a crocodile leaped out at him. Scrooge jumped back just in time!

That night, Scrooge and Glomgold heard someone open their cell door.

"Leave quietly!" whispered Sherwebazad. "I have put the guards to sleep to help you escape."

"But how?" asked Scrooge, following her.

"I told them a story. Whenever I tell a story, it puts everyone to sleep. Come," she said, leading the way. "I'll help you sneak out of the city."

23

Meanwhile, Huey, Dewey and Louie were keeping an eye on the Genie. "We have to get him back into the Magic Lamp," whispered Huey. "Something tells me that Unca Scrooge won't be able to come home until we do." His brothers agreed, and together they went to the Genie.

"We've been thinking," began Louie. "The way you've been eating, you're probably too fat to fit into the lamp."

"Oh, yes, I can!" said the Genie. Once he was back inside the lamp, Dewey plugged it up tight.

"Hurray! We did it!" yelled the boys.

Once he was back in the lamp, the Genie lost his powers. The spell over Scrooge and Glomgold was broken.

Seven days after the race began, a tired Scrooge McDuck dragged himself up to the door of the Hot Ice Cream parlor.

"You're a little late, friend!" bragged Glomgold, holding the Magic Lamp.

"You didn't win fairly," said Scrooge. "When your partners came looking for you, you left me stranded in the desert!"

Glomgold unstoppered the lamp, and the Genie appeared. "What is your first wish?" he asked.

"That Scrooge be left alone on a desert island," Glomgold replied. Immediately, Scrooge disappeared.

"Ha, ha, ha!" laughed Glomgold. "I wish I could be there to see his face!"

"That's your second wish!" said the Genie, and Glomgold found himself on the island with Scrooge.

"Oh, no!" cried Glomgold. "I wish I had never found this stupid lamp!" Instantly, Scrooge and Glomgold were back in Aladdin's cave.

Once again, Scrooge McDuck and Flintheart Glomgold were face to face, where they had first found the Magic Lamp. But this time, there was no lamp.

Glomgold's dynamite had made a big hole at the end of the cave. The walls of the cave began to crack, and rocks were falling everywhere. Scrooge and Glomgold raced for the exit. Once outside, Glomgold ran away.

31

"Are you all right, Unca Scrooge?" asked Huey.

"Aye, but I nearly left me feathers in there. And all to find an empty cave!"

"Are we going back home, then?" asked Dewey. "It's hot here, and we'd really like a good swim in the pool."

* * *

Inside Aladdin's cave, under a pile of rocks, glowed the Magic Lamp. The Genie would have to wait another 400 years before someone would find it again.

SEND IN THE CLONES

Scrooge McDuck owed all his wealth to his lucky dime, Old Number One. His enemy, the witch Magica de Spell, wanted that dime, and she asked the Beagle Boys to help her get it.

"I want you to steal Old Number One, and nothing else," said Magica, standing outside Scrooge's mansion. "Nothing else!" she hissed.

The witch cast a magic spell and a sparkling cloud fell over the Beagle Boys. When the cloud was gone, the Beagle Boys looked just like Huey, Dewey and Louie.

"Perfect!" laughed Magica. "You look just like Scrooge McDuck's nephews. Now go! Bring me back Old Number One!"

"Don't worry, chief!" said Big Time Beagle.

"Remember," ordered Magica. "Stay away from mirrors. They'll show who you really are."

Once inside, the disguised Beagle Boys ran into Scrooge. He was surprised to see them.

"I thought you were at the movies," he said. "Well, never mind. An important reporter is comin' to interview me, so be good boys, all right?" The Beagles nodded and ran upstairs.

Just then, someone rang the doorbell. It was Mary Query, the reporter from *Ducksweek*.

"Welcome to me humble home!" said Scrooge.

"I hope you'll just be yourself," said the reporter. "There's no need to put on a show for me."

Upstairs, the Beagle Boys started looking for Old Number One. "Let's start in Scrooge's office," said Baby Face.

They found a safe set into the floor, underneath the rug. Big Time blew it open with dynamite. But the explosion blew the floor open, too. The safe and the Beagle Boys crashed down to the first floor.

At that very moment, Mrs. Beakley, the housekeeper, walked into the room.

"What's going on here?" she asked. "I thought your uncle asked you to behave!"

Right behind the disguised Beagle Boys was a mirror. When Mrs. Beakley looked into it, she saw who they really were. The poor lady screamed.

"Grab her!" yelled Big Time.

Meanwhile, the real Huey, Dewey, and Louie were coming home from the movies.

They met their uncle and the reporter in the hall.

"Didn't I tell you to behave?" asked Scrooge. "I just heard Mrs. Beakley scream. What have you been up to?"

"But, Unca Scrooge, we weren't here. We just got back from the movies," said Huey.

"Boil me bagpipes! I've never heard such a lie! What must Miss Query think? Go to your room!"

"Having that reporter here must be making Unca Scrooge nervous," said Louie, as they headed for the kitchen. "Better not argue with him. Let's see if we can find any snacks."

Meanwhile Burger Beagle had stopped in the kitchen to raid the refrigerator. He was just about to start on a chocolate cake when Scrooge's nephews walked in. They could hardly believe their eyes.

"Hey! He looks just like Huey!" said a surprised Louie.

"Who is this fake?" asked Huey.

"You're the fake!" replied Burger. "I'm the real Huey."

Burger Beagle didn't fool anyone. The three brothers took him to their bedroom and tied him up.

"I'm going to get Unca Scrooge," said the real Huey. "You two try to find out why he's pretending to be me."

Huey left the room. A minute later, Scrooge walked in. The reporter took one look at the fake Huey, all tied up, and quickly took a few pictures for her newspaper.

"What kind of game is this?" asked Scrooge, ashamed of his nephews. "What will Miss Query think?"

Meanwhile, Magica de Spell thought that the Beagle Boys were taking too long to find Old Number One.

"Those boys are only going to make things worse!" she said to herself. "I'll have to find that coin myself."

In moments Magica looked exactly like Mrs. Beakley.

"There!" said the witch. "I can look for the coin and no one will bother me. And since the real Mrs. Beakley is locked up in the shed, there won't be two Mrs. Beakleys wandering around."

Magica looked everywhere she could think of for Scrooge's lucky dime. When she walked into the library, her heart skipped a beat. There, sitting on a shelf in a glass case, was Old Number One!

"It's mine, at last!" she cried. Then she heard someone enter the library.

"I've found it," she said to the little duck in the red shirt. "Let's get out of here."

But the little duck was the real Huey, not Burger Beagle.

Something about Mrs. Beakley bothered Huey. Could she be a fake, too? He decided to follow her. She led him into the shed, and Huey knew that he was right. The fake Dewey and Louie were guarding the real Mrs. Beakley.

"Let's get out of here fast," ordered Magica, turning back into her real self. "By the time they find out what we've done, we'll be back at my hideout, safe and sound."

They locked Mrs. Beakley back up in the shed, and raced for the helicopter that was waiting for them.

After they took off, Magica turned her partners back into the Beagle Boys. But the one they called Burger didn't turn back, because he was the real Huey.

"Lightning and thunder!" Magica cried. "This is one of Scrooge's nephews! Burger must still be at the house!"

Meanwhile, the fake Huey had turned back into Burger Beagle. The reporter snapped his picture.

"What is the meanin' of this?" yelled Scrooge. "Tell us what's goin' on right now, or we'll leave you tied up for three weeks with no food!"

Burger couldn't stand the thought of going without food for so long, so he told them everything.

Scrooge and the others rushed off to rescue Huey.

Magica, meanwhile, was testing the coin she had taken from Scrooge's mansion. It wasn't Old Number One.

Suddenly Scrooge broke into the hideout. "Let me nephew go!" he ordered.

"First, give me Old Number One," said Magica. "The one I took was a fake. If you love your nephew," she said, "you'll give me the right coin!"

"I'll give you Burger for Huey," offered Scrooge.

"Keep him!" said Magica. "He's of no use to me."

Scrooge thought about trying to rescue his nephew by force, but it was no use. The witch had too many magic powers, and the Beagle Boys could be dangerous.

"You win," said Scrooge, handing her a coin.

"Mine at last!" Magica cried.

Huey ran into his uncle's arms.

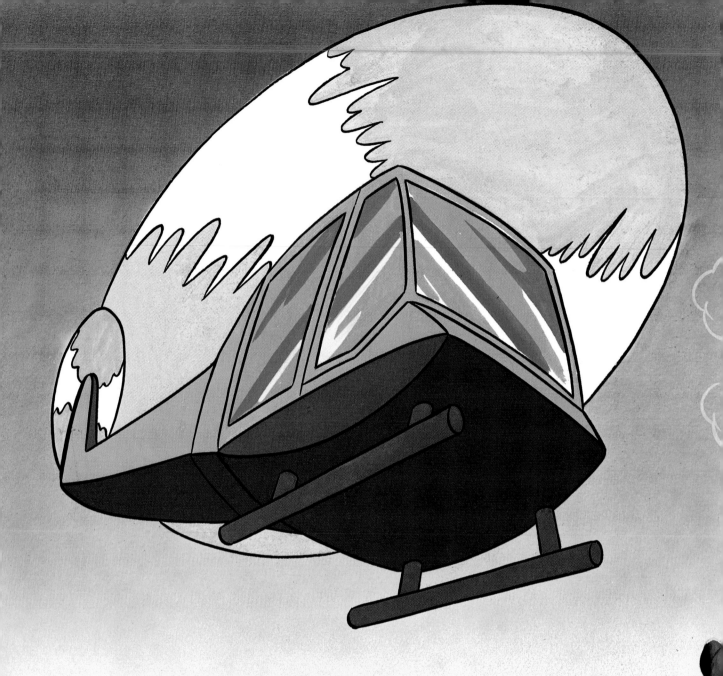

"Let's get out of here," said Scrooge.

The Beagle Boys let them go. They were celebrating. Burger was the happiest because he didn't have to worry about going without food for three weeks. He danced around, bumping into tables and knocking Magica's potions over. Soon the room was filled with smoke.

From their helicopter, Scrooge and the others watched Magica's hideout explode.

"Magica kept your good luck coin, but I don't think it helped her," said the reporter.

Scrooge laughed and took a coin from his pocket.

"I never gave her the real Old Number One," said Scrooge. "I kept it for meself!"

"Hurray for Unca Scrooge!" they all shouted.

64